BEDTIME for MAZIKS

Yael Levy

illustrated by **Nabila Adani**

KAR-BEN
PUBLISHING

When the moon has gone to bed,
and the sun pokes out its head,

love and laughter catch and spread
by *maziks* who begin their day.

Do they rumble?

Do they fight?

Do they snarl with all their might?

Are they just a scary sight?

What do *maziks* do each day?

When they're messy, playing rough,
making trouble, breaking stuff . . .
some call them imps and say, "Enough!"
Is that what *maziks* do each day?

Do they play outside for hours,
charging up and down tall towers?

Do they have great magic powers?
What do *maziks* do each day?

Do they swim and belly flop
till the lifeguard tells them, "STOP!"
Do they laugh until they drop?
What do *maziks* do each day?

When they play with games and toys,
there's racing, teasing, lots of noise,
and jokes that everyone enjoys.
Is that what *maziks* do each day?

Do they share their challah bread,
spill their juice, and (once they're fed) . . .

. . . have grand pillow fights in bed?

Is that how *maziks* end their day?

When the moon is bold and bright,
and the sun has slipped from sight,
little monsters say, "Good night."
That's how *maziks* end their day.

Say "Sh'ma," get tucked in bed,
kisses planted on each head,
dreams that glide on starlit thread—
that's how *maziks* end their day.

About the Author
Author Yael Levy loves creating books for children. Her work has been published in a variety of places, including the *Jerusalem Post*. She lives in Atlanta, Georgia.

About the Illustrator
Nabila Adani was born and grew up in Jakarta, Indonesia. The illustrator of many picture books, she first got the idea to illustrate children's books while looking for an Indonesian picture book for her son. She lives in Indonesia.

BEDTIME for MAZIKS

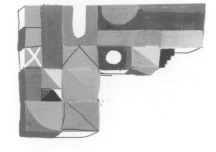

Mazik is a Yiddish word for a devilish imp or a rambunctious mischief-maker. Exasperated by the tumult of a child's creative self-expression, parents might lovingly call this child a *mazik*.

Thank you Aroma Writers, my family, and all the *maziks*, everywhere. You are loved. – Y.L.

KAR-BEN PUBLISHING®
An imprint of Lerner Publishing Group, Inc.
241 First Avenue North
Minneapolis, MN 55401 USA

Website address: www.karben.com

Main body text set in Billy Infant Regular.
Typeface provided by Sparkytype.

Library of Congress Cataloging-in-Publication Data

Names: Levy, Yael, 1971– author. | Adani, Nabila, 1991– illustrator.
Title: Bedtime for maziks / by Yael Levy ; [illustrated by Nabila Adani].
Description: Minneapolis, MN : Kar-Ben Publishing, an imprint of Lerner Publishing Group, Inc., 2022. | Audience: Ages 4–9. | Audience: Grades K–1. | Summary: "After a day of roly-poly fun and shenanigans, it's bedtime for maziks, the Yiddish word for pranksters or little mischief-makers, a name Jewish parents may lovingly call their rambunctious little ones"— Provided by publisher.
Identifiers: LCCN 2021014670 (print) | LCCN 2021014671 (ebook) | ISBN 9781728424279 | ISBN 9781728427942 (paperback) | ISBN 9781728444215 (ebook)
Subjects: CYAC: Stories in rhyme. | Behavior—Fiction. | Bedtime—Fiction. | Jews—Fiction.
Classification: LCC PZ8.3.L582 Be 2022 (print) | LCC PZ8.3.L582 (ebook) | DDC [E]—dc23

LC record available at https://lccn.loc.gov/2021014670
LC ebook record available at https://lccn.loc.gov/2021014671

Manufactured in the United States of America
1-49297-49413-6/22/2021